Juice Box

RICKY BOONE

Andrea Johnson Books Publishing

Other books by Ricky Boone

Pillow Talk

Stay tuned for more books by Ricky Boone Coming soon!

Guns and Butter

The Bouquet

Visit the publishing website to find out more about Ricky Boone's upcoming books. www.Ajbpublishing.com

Ricky Boone

Juice Box

Cover art designed by Andrea Johnson Books Publishing.

First published by Andrea Johnson Books Publishing. 04/29/2020

6565 N. MacArthur Blvd, Suite 225 Dallas, TX. 75039
www.Ajbpublishing.com

ISBN: 978-0-578-67628-9

Juice Box

Acknowledgements

I would like to acknowledge all of those who believed and motivated me. As far as: Pammy Budd, the mother of my child. My mother, Dorothy Osborne. My aunt Bonita Brown, and Diana Buford. My brother, Jonathon Boone James and sister, Jaylene Osborne, my brother Kevin Wicker, and sister, Brandy Brown.

A lot of close friends, Brandon Mackey, Marcus Grey, (Focus) My two sons, Keaveon and Sencier Boone, who read a lot of my material and showed support. Janae Abney and the many faces of fans and family who's supported and have shown lots of love.

And I would like to thank Andrea Johnson for helping to make all this happen.

What inspired me to write this book came mostly from a relationship I was in, and the woman I had dealings with. All the poems and letters that I'd written to her, and posted on social media, prompted my fans to suggest the writing of this story.

- Ricky Boone

TABLE OF CONTENTS

CHAPTER ONE – LOST POTENTIAL...........8

CHAPTER TW0 – THE SEED OF SEDUCTION...................................22

CHAPTER THREE – THE BINDING...........30

CHAPTER FOUR – THE REVELATIONS....37

CHAPTER FIVE – UNHEALTHY SOUL TIES......49

CHAPTER SIX – THE CONVERSATION....61

CHAPTER SEVEN – SUCCUBUS............69

Lost Potential

~ In life, there are no coincidences ~

Chapter One

Lonnie McGill's thoughts took shape, as he remembered that fateful day...

"I met her at a night club in 97 called, The Juice Box. It was sort of an accident. Me and my homeboys were playing around, until one of my idiot friends approached one of the girls that I actually liked. Which so happened to be her. Her name was KeeKe. But they called her, Lady Bug.'"

Lonnie recalled the events as if they happened yesterday...

***

She was dancing to the latest hit by Rome, 'I belong to you.' It was as if her body moved in slow motion. Up and down the walls, as the lights kept flashing on and off. But the main thing that made her stand out the most...was that booty.

"I'm a go tell her you want to get with cuz." Said Joe. Joe was one of the main ones who'd talk to just about anybody with a pretty face.

"I'm good." Said Lonnie McGill.

"Nigga you scared?" Replied Joe.

"No." Said Lonnie. "I just don't want her to say the wrong thing, and I spazz out on her, due to she looks stuck up."

"Whatever, homie." Joe replied. "You do you, and sit up here lonely with all these niggaz, while fantasizing about her."

But Joe was right at that time. Lonnie was afraid of rejection. But like all bone heads, Joe went up to her anyway, and told her Lonnie wanted her.

Lady Bug walked over to the table and just sat there, staring at Lonnie. And for a split second, she paused and said, "what's up?"

Lonnie immediately froze with no words to say, due to all the trash talking he'd done with his boys. The opportunity was finally here, and presented itself.

She presented herself and said her name was 'Kenyana,' but people call her. 'KeeKe.'

"Well what's good, KeeKe?" Lonnie finally dredged up the nerve to respond. "I'm Lonnie, from Saginaw. Nice to meet you."

Just her smile alone had Lonnie zoned out. But it's what she had on that made him breathless.

Her thighs, her booty, her breasts, kept his thoughts in the air.

If she could only read his mind, she wouldn't even be there. But already married to him, and in the bed butt naked, having every part of her body sucked on.

"Damn! You're staring hard. What are you thinking about?" Said KeeKe.

Lonnie was quicker on his feet this time.

"I'm just fascinated by your beauty." He replied.

And it was from that moment, things took off from there.

***

Three weeks later, the two were closer than ever. It was almost like they knew each other for months at the time. They shared secrets, deep things about one another. She shared personal things with him that she never really told a guy, in such a short period of time before. About being abused. Molested. Her child's father being homeless. This woman had a lot going on. However, Lonnie was falling extremely in love with her, after only three weeks. He began to believe it was love at first sight.

Until one night, Lonnie received a call from KeeKe.

"What you doin'?" She asked him.

Lonnie replied with a smirk, "nothing right now, but just sittin up here with Joe smokin a blunt, relaxing. Why, what's up?"

"I just want you to come over." KeeKe responded. "I'm feelin some type of way right now, and I'm alone and my son's asleep."

Right then and there, Lonnie knew what was up.

"Oh yeah...so you want me to slide through for the night..."

"But slide through and sleep in me." KeeKe finished his statement with a soft whisper.

"Oh really?" Said Lonnie, feeling her vibes through the phone.

"Yes really." KeeKe replied. "So you're on your way? I'm sitting here with a big T-shirt on, and nothing up under it."

"I'm on my way right now." Lonnie said without hesitation. He left Joe at the house and jumped into his car, headed down Dixie Highway. He was there within fifteen minutes.

As he pulled up, he paused and thought to himself for a moment. That this could change everything, if he went forward and slept with her. He had a small prickle of doubt enter his mind, but then quickly dismissed it.

Lonnie hopped out of the car, checked his wallet for the rubbers that he'd stashed in there, and headed to the front door. But just as he was about to ring the doorbell, she answered it.

"Hey you." KeeKe said with a smile.

"Hey..." Lonnie replied, taking in her appearance.

"I thought you were gonna back out, after I saw you sittin in my driveway all zoned out."

"Me? Back out? Stop playin' girl." Lonnie chuckled easily, trying to gather his thoughts. He swallowed deep, looking at her fat luscious booty twerking on its own, as she walked into the house, headed for the couch.

'Oh my god.' Lonnie thought to himself.

"You like what you see?" KeeKe said seductively.

"Do I?" Lonnie replied with a smooth approach.

"I'm a just keep it blunt with you." Said KeeKe. "I don't want to do much talking. We can talk later.

You and I know what you came over here to do. My baby is sleep. So let's head into my room and get things popping."

They headed into her room and slightly closed the door. The black boy shorts she had on was such a sight. Lonnie walked over to her, as he stared into her sexy bedroom eyes.

"What you gonna do with all this?" KeeKe said softly.

Lonnie began to slowly pull her shorts down. As he marveled at her beautiful shaved juice box, she said to him...

"Tell me how sweet I taste."

KeeKe placed her fingers into herself, then placed them slowly into his mouth.

"Am I sweet?" She asked him.

Lonnie licked the moisture off of her fingers. "Very." He replied.

"Then taste the rest of me." KeeKe said, highly aroused now.

She laid down onto the bed and stretched out on her back, spreading her legs over her shoulders.

Lonnie moved into her body, and placed his full lips onto her exposed and waiting, dripping flesh. Inhaling her juice box. He placed one finger in her anal, and the other deep into her box.

As the spit began to flow between the cracks, running down the sheets with no towels on the bed, it left all sorts of wet spots. It was lust tangled into love, and a moment between them giving to one another, and the sloppy head that was exchanged in passion.

Lonnie was gasping for air, as she pushed his face deeper and deeper into a sweeter taste.

Taking control, Lonnie tossed her legs even higher, and thrust himself deeper into her outer space. She was the type that loved to make love with the lights on, so you could see the expressions on her face.

Slow circles were causing the juices to flow. He pulled back, and fed her just a little, then sank into her some more.

Then KeeKe changed the tempo, and climbed on top. She licked her lips, then just drops. Grinding his love real slow, then suddenly stopped. She turned around and faced the wall, while her back was facing him.

The night was young, but moving fast, even though the motions were slow. Tears were falling from her eyes, cause the love making had never felt so good. She was now bending over, showing that she's a little hood.

Body was clapping on his piece pipe with the perfect angle. Gripping the sheets and on the pillow she was biting. The pressure and the pleasure were unbearable, as she began to rain and explode on him. It was unforgettable. From the bed, to the walls, to the floor, to the stairway. They made love multiple times, tasting one another. Juices and all.

***

"Wow." Said Lonnie. "Where do we go from here?"

"Wherever you wanna go." KeeKe replied, as her head lay gently on his tattooed chest, with her hands softly caressing his v-line.

"I can just lay here with you like this forever." Said Lonnie.

"You don't have to go. You can stay here for the night." KeeKe spoke while caressing his chest.

Everything seemed perfect. But you see, what Lonnie didn't know was that KeeKe had some issues that he'd overlooked. What she'd never told him, was why she'd never been able to hold onto a relationship. But he would soon find out.

"So we gonna seal this and make it official." Said Lonnie.

KeeKe smiled and replied. "Baby, it was always official. It was really sealed the moment you entered into me."

"Oh damn! The second I entered you?" Lonnie replied with a smirk.

"Nigga, the very second you entered me." KeeKe responded to him with a straight face.

"I got you, love." Said Lonnie. "One thing you don't have to worry about, is me playing with your heart. I'm one hundred with you, no games. Just don't turn on me."

As they covered each other gracefully, holding each other in their arms, underneath the fan as the sweat dried from their bodies, running down to the wet sheets. They fell asleep.

***

The next morning the alarm went off...

Errrr....errrr...errr.....

"Jesus! We're late!" Lonnie shouted. They hopped out of the bed butt naked, knowing that they both worked on the same schedule. But KeeKe had to stop to drop off her child at school first.

Lonnie got dressed and jetted out the door, shouting out loud behind him, "I'll see you later on, baby!" He quickly headed home to hit the shower and change clothes, then head off to work.

Lonnie's thoughts were in a maze as he silently said to himself, "damn! What a night! It would have been nice to have actually gotten some good loving in the morning, but I probably would've been exhausted, and no good at work."

The moment Lonnie entered the building that he worked in, he headed to the lunch room to get his morning coffee.

An old lady was sitting at one of the tables near him, watching him stir his sugars and cream together. As he sipped off the stir stick, taste testing it, she silently said...

"Ooooweeeee......she's so sweet, isn't she? But everything that is sweet, isn't so good to eat."

Lonnie turned around, confused.

"Excuse me?" He asked her.

The woman responded immediately. "You really don't know. You don't know what you've locked yourself into, do you?"

"Lady what are you talking about?" Lonnie replied, starting to get freaked out.

"Besides, who are you? When did you even start working here? I've never seen you here before."

The woman smiled slowly and said, "does it matter?" She had white pearly teeth, and dark Hershey skin. She looked as if she was from another country. She had long jet-black braided hair, with a foreign accent.

"You slept with Succubus."

"Who the hell is Succubus?" Lonnie questioned her, feeling the tension beginning to prickle down his back.

The old woman smiled and replied to him. "She's been watching you for a long time, Lonnie."

"Watching me? How? And how do you know my name?" Lonnie asked, his alarm starting to grow.

"Watching you in your sleep. Your dreams, your heart. And in many ways, what you desire most. You let her in at an early age." The woman explained to him.

"How did I let whoever you're talking about in, with your crazy ass, at an early age?" Lonnie replied sarcastically.

"Pictures, magazines, books, music, and most of all pornography." The old woman said to him, as she stood up in Lonnie's face and blew a cold wind of her breath onto him.

It was then that Lonnie was able to see the flashbacks, on how it all began. And the seed of seduction that had been planted.

The Seed of Seduction

- You will reap what you sow -

Chapter two

It was 1992, that year was hot, and music was jumping. People had the barbecue grills lit up, while the children ran around the yard, playing tag, or having water balloon fights.

"Girl, we goin' get you out of that mess you in." Said Dottie. Dottie was Lonnie's mother, and was very outspoken.

"You can come stay with us, until you get yourself together." Dottie was talking to her best friend, Liz, who was going through an abusive relationship with her and her kids.

She had an older son named Kenneth, and a younger son who was the baby, named Dre. Kenneth was only fourteen years old, and Dre was just four months. During that time, Kenneth would hang out and introduce things to Lonnie and his little brother, Sadell.

Weeks later, Liz and her children moved in. Liz had the guest room, and Kenneth shared the room with Lonnie and Sadell.

You see, Lonnie was younger than Kenneth. He was only twelve at the time. And Kenneth was far more advanced in things, due to being exposed to them at an early age.

Shortly after moving in, while Kenneth was unpacking, he approached Lonnie...

"Hey, want to help me unpack me and my mother's things?" Said Kenneth.

"Sure." Lonnie replied. "You'll get done a bit faster. Then maybe we can have time to play the game before it's too late."

It must have been at least twenty boxes that needed to be sorted out. Plus they took time to set up the television and VCR.

"Man, I want you to check something out real quick." Said Kenneth. "So lock the door, cause we can get in a lot of trouble if caught." Kenneth pulled out a video tape that had no name or title on it, and popped it into the VCR.

Instantly the boys were glued, like they were in a trance. Lonnie and his little brother were like, what the heck is this? All the while, Kenneth was in the back laying on the bed, enjoying it like a regular home movie.

"It's a porno." Said Kenneth, with pride. He laughed so hard at the two of them that tears fell from his eyes, because he knew they had no clue at what they were watching.

"Let me tell you what you do, in the process of watching this." Said Kenneth.

He sat back and was glued to the screen. Mind blown and aroused, as they watched all the sucking and grinding, and moaning on the television set.

"Have you all ever masturbated, jack off, choke your chicken, or beat your meat?" He asked them.

Lonnie replied in confusion.

"No. What's that?"

As Kenneth once again started laughing, he slowly grabbed a hold of his mother's hair jam and started explaining what it was.

"You get your Johnson all greased up, and your palms. And you place yourself into your hands, like this. And then move in motion while you watch the movie." Then he began to demonstrate.

The shows got longer later on in the weeks. The boys started finding themselves disappearing for long periods of time. Sneaking off to watch the porno. Their minds were now flooded at an early age, with nothing but sex.

From hair gels, to conditioners, to Vaseline, those items never lasted long anymore. There was no baby oil or lotion in the house. And as the years increased, the addiction got worse.

Lonnie was now fifteen years old. Masturbating daily, almost eight times a day. Anything would trigger his sex drive off on television. To music videos, and even songs. Jet magazines even set his fire off.

But Lonnie was afraid to have sex physically, because of the fear of diseases and pregnancy. So releasing himself in the shower or on the toilet, was a must.

This was something that he had a problem with. Not knowing that a spirit had attached itself to him. It fell upon him the moment he opened the gates, by watching that first porno Kenneth had exposed him to.

It had gotten to the point that by just listening to a woman's voice, he could imagine how she would sound during sex. He could picture women without their clothes on, in public.

He quickly picked up a fetish for thick lips and thighs. And seductive eyes, and a bubble back side that would blow your mind. He loved it nasty, sloppy, but still never had physical sex yet. But his imagination was X-rated. And watching those porns had shaped it.

Until one day, he met a woman that forever changed his life. Her name was, Cookie.

Cookie was a very attractive woman who loved to deal with thugs. And Lonnie just happened to be at the right place and the right time.

He was hanging with his cousins, Chris, J-rock, and Dirt. Who smoked blunts like it was breakfast, lunch and dinner. Dirt stayed on the block with a pocket full of stones, as well as money, right along with Chris. However, Dirt was one you had to be very careful with, due to he kept a 35 on him at all times.

"Nigga, come and help me bag this yolk up." Said Dirt. Sitting in the kitchen in a cloud of smoke, surrounded by bricks of weed chopped up on the table with stones, and empty Newport boxes.

"Roll up, cuz." Said Chris. As Dirt rolled up, they sat and joked at the table. Talking about one another's flaws, clothes, and stupidest moments.

Lonnie hung around them due to the fact they were family. But they stayed surrounded by all types of women. Whether they were white, black, mexican, whatever. Even fat girls got love.

They were a bunch of teenagers that would use blunts for bait. To draw in females that would sex in the same room, like a big orgy. At the same time, the blunt was passed around. That's when Lonnie met Cookie.

Cookie was off limits. At least she was supposed to be. She was connected to the plug, which was very known around that time.

"That's some good weed. Pass the 'B' over this way." Said Cookie.

Cookie knew that Lonnie had a thing for her. But out of respect, he never cut off into her, due to who she was connect to.

"Man, I'm high as hell." Said Lonnie. Passing the blunt across the table to Cookie. Watching Chris with the craziest smirk on his face, like ooweee, as the blunt circled the table.

The binding

- Be careful the ties that bind -

Chapter Three

Two weeks later, Lonnie was on a weed run, and was told Cookie had it, and headed over to her place.

Now where he was headed at, he had no business on that side of town. Due to the people he rolled with was from a different set, as far as gang territory. But he went anyway over to Cookie's, eager to get a sac to smoke with his boys. And in the process of him being there, he stayed there a little too long, and things happened.

However, Lonnie didn't care anymore. Even though it could have cost him his life.

Cookie did some things to him that he'd never experienced before. Not knowing Cookie was a Creole woman. She tampered with a lot of things concerning voodoo. Especially when it came to being sexual.

Lonnie left out of her home never being the same again. There was a connection that was there that kept his mind in the wind. He couldn't get her out of his head. He woke up, ate, slept, worked, with nothing but her on his mind. All he could feel and think of, was when was the next time he could possibly see her again.

"Hey cuz." Dirt said to him one day. "You and Cookie been sort of actin funny toward each other when she falls through. What's goin on?"

"We good, cuz." Lonnie replied. "Ain't nothing poppin. I just been having a lot on my mind, that's all."

"Her, right?" Dirt said sarcastically. "You know you can't touch that. But for some reason, Nigga, it's more to it than you're telling me. I know you, what's good? Talk to me."

"You wouldn't believe me if I told you." Lonnie replied solemnly.

"Try me, Nigga." Dirt continued to press him.

Lonnie relented, and just came out with it.

"I smashed."

Dirt broke out in laughter. "Fool, yeah right!" He mocked him.

"I slept with her a week ago, going over there to get some smoke." Said Lonnie.

"Are you serious?!" Dirt was shocked.

"Dead serious. We sat and chilled for a moment, she rolled up and started talking crazy. Next thing I knew her head was in my lap, and we were making a connection like we was making a porno."

"Hell naw, cuz! Wow!" Dirt shouted. "You better keep that hidden under the rug."

And as they kept discussing what went down, while Lonnie was going into heavy detail, his phone started ringing, and he sent it straight to voicemail.

He knew it was Cookie looking for him, because she was alone once more. So he checked his message privately, and listened to her sultry voice.

"What's good, baby? You dodging me? Get at me. I gotta itch that's in need of scratching." 'Click'

Weeks went into months. Almost close to a year. Lonnie found himself back and forth sleeping with Cookie on the low. However at the same time, Cookie was still messing around with her plug.

Lonnie was hooked, due to the fact that first off, Cookie was an older woman. And he was only eighteen. She was a cougar compared to him, she being thirty eight. Cookie knew exactly how to get Lonnie, and it was through his pants, a blunt, and a blowjob. She could get Lonnie to shoot up a school park if she wanted to. She had him gone off of her juice box.

She had the craziest control over him. To the point he started selling dope for her. It was almost like she was a queen pin. Her box kept him smoked mentally. Sexually and spiritually.

Until one night, Lonnie got a call from Cookie stating some of the most devastating news ever. It had him so twisted, he almost wanted to kill himself.

That fateful night plays a big part in why Lonnie thinks the way he does to this very day.

That night, the phone rang...

"Hello..."

"Hey, we need to talk." It was Cookie.

"Ok. What's good?" Said Lonnie.

"Julian knows we've been messing around." Cookie blurted out.

Julian was the plug, and also Cookie's boyfriend.

"How he find out?!" Lonnie shouted in shock.

"He's been tracing our calls, back and forth to one another." Cookie replied.

"Damn, straight up." Lonnie mumbled.

"All I'm saying baby, is stay strapped. And by the way, I'm pregnant, and it's between you and him."

Lonnie went into complete silence.

Now with possibly a baby on the way, until further notice, the goal was to stay alive. This is what Lonnie was thinking. He'd been sleeping with Cookie for close to a year now, and there was no telling how long that Nigga been knowing. And if he knows his whereabouts.

But that didn't stop Lonnie from sleeping with Cookie. He just kept that 357 up under his pillow whenever he found himself at her place.

This was the growth of that spirit Cookie carried that latched itself onto Lonnie.

Succubus. Cookie carried many spirits as well. Controlling, manipulating, sexual. However, Lonnie just couldn't let those heavy thighs go.

The Revelations

- *There is more that lies within you* -

Chapter Four

Lonnie suddenly snapped out of his hypnosis, and seeing his past, and realized he was back in the lunch room with the old lady.

"What the freak! What the hell did you just do to me?!" Lonnie shouted at the woman, dazed and confused.

The old woman smiled. "You remember now, don't you?" She said quietly.

"So you're saying this is a spirit, a demon I picked up during my upbringing?"

"Yes." Replied the woman. "This explains why you have the urge to always have relations with anything that you find, that looks good to you. People with this spirit connects very strongly to you, and you feel it. And it can kill you."

The old woman continued to warn him.

"You are addicted to the juice box. Cookie did something to you, and whatever was in her has never left you. Because she latched onto you. But now, it has met with an unfamiliar spirit that is within KeeKe."

She smiled and looked at Lonnie, shaking her head knowingly, and chuckled.

"Ha, ha, ha, so young and dumb." She said ominously. She pointed her finger at him and his groin, and said...

"You were thinking with the wrong head."

***

"You coming over later?" Lonnie heard the voice speaking softly into the phone, lost for words after what he'd experienced earlier with the old lady.

"Huh?" Lonnie replied, still trying to gather his wits.

The voice on the phone repeated itself, sounding a little more persistent this time. It was KeeKe.

"Are you coming over later?" She said again.

"Yeah, yeah." Lonnie finally responded.

"You good?" KeeKe asked.

"Yeah, I'm good. I'm just thrown off a bit. I met this weird freaky old lady, that's it. But I'll be over."

As Lonnie continued throughout his day at work, mind blown and thinking about his past, he began to mull over things that he'd thought were long buried.

Because he never did find out about the baby situation with Cookie, since she'd skipped town, and it's been close to fifteen years since he'd heard anything from her. And truth be told, Julian, which was her plug, just mysteriously ended up disappearing. Well in other words, dead.

He was found on the railroad tracks with two bullet holes in his head, and one in his chest. Which was still an unsolved murder to this day.

At the end of his shift, Lonnie took off and headed over to KeeKe's house.

"Hey baby, you on your way over?" KeeKe called and asked him.

"Yes, I'm on my way as we speak." Said Lonnie.

"Well I'm a be in the shower when you pull up, due to I'm all sticky, and I need to freshen up."

Lonnie envisioned this with a smile.

"Ok, well I'll be there in about five minutes. Is it anything you want while I'm out?"

"No. I'm good, love. Just get here, I miss you already." KeeKe replied.

Lonnie finally pulled up and headed inside the house. The door was unlocked so he was able to walk right in.

Coming in, he could hear the shower running as he headed upstairs. And as soon as he turned the corner, he saw her.

She was bent over in a perfect arch, and still soaking wet from the shower. Lonnie walked over to her, his steps measured, as he unbuttoned his shirt.

He approached her while she was still arched up in perfect formation, and he dropped down to his knees to taste every bit of her juice.

As the water fell down from her nipples, and she rocked back and forth into his mouth, while he sucked on her moist lips from behind, a tear fell from her eye, as KeeKe was bombarded with how good he was making her feel. It was unbearable, and hard to swallow.

As Lonnie placed two fingers into both holes, the steam from the shower began to seep out of the bathroom. Making it hotter in the bedroom.

He flipped her over and onto her back, placing her feet behind her head. Touching the headboard.

Spitting, and spitting, and spitting, and swallowing her soul. Now she was halfway off the bed, pretty much facing him upside down. While he was off the bed standing up, placing himself into her mouth, full of spit.

"You so nasty." Lonnie said with his eyes closed in pleasure.

"But you like it..." KeeKe replied, as she gagged, her eyes watering from the passion and pressure.

Lonnie pulled back.

"Arch that pretty thing back up in the air for me." He told her.

She slowly arched over and stretched out, spreading open her love as he entered all of himself into her.

"You feel that." Said Lonnie, as he saw her biting down on the pillow, gripping the sheets.

Pop, pop, smack, smack! Was the only sound that was heard, with each thrust and pound.

He pulled back and sucked on her some more. Then flipped her over to the side, then onto her back, giving her straight eye contact as she yelled out, "Yes baby! Like that! Oowee...boy...I love you."

Lonnie pounded into her while the shower was still running. Sweat was now pouring down his face as he pumped faster, as he could feel her cumming.

"Boy..ohhhh....I love you..." KeeKe repeated her words. And Lonnie looked at her. Suddenly her face distorted into Cookie's.

"Damn! What the..." Lonnie freaked out, completely taken off guard.

Meanwhile KeeKe was still so zoned out, and into the love making, that she didn't realize his motion had just shifted.

Pushing aside that brief moment of insanity, Lonnie bent her back over and spit in between her butt cheeks. Then went straight into her anal. She gagged and took in a deep breath.

"Oh shhhh..." KeeKe cried out in surprise and pleasure, having never experienced that before.

You see, Lonnie had done all these things with Cookie. So in his mind, he was out for more.

"Take it...take it." Lonnie ordered her, as he gave her a little bit more, inch after inch. "Stop running, you just gonna be a little bit sore."

"Oh my god..." KeeKe gasped out. Something was about to happen, that had never occurred to her before. She was about to have multiple orgasms, and was soaking everything onto the floor.

Lonnie eventually got his in.

"Ooooweeee.... This was a bit different. What's got into you?" KeeKe asked him.

"I really don't know." Lonnie replied, as he undressed. Fully taking off his soaking shirt that was drenched in sweat. The shower was still running, and had been for the past thirty three to forty minutes.

"I'm a hop in this shower." He said to her. Hoping there was still hot water left. All sticky and sweaty, KeeKe decided to join him.

***

Hours later, after they both showered, ate dinner, and relaxed a bit, they put the baby to bed and made sure he was cozy and fed. It was eight pm. And Lonnie wanted to catch up to Joe and see what was up before he checked in, being it's been a minute since they'd hung out.

"Yo cuz, where you at?" Said Lonnie.

"What's good my nigga, you know where I be, get at me." Said Joe.

Joe was at the spot which was the bar. The same place where he met KeeKe. So he decided to head down there. He figured he'd have a couple of beers with him before he checked in for the night.

Pulling up at the bar he noticed something that was quite weird. He felt a scratch on his back that kept irritating him, and it burned. He figured maybe it was the cologne that wasn't agreeing with his skin. Causing it to react that way.

However, he headed into the club anyway, and ran into the old lady from his workplace, once again.

Lonnie didn't want to know what a woman like her was even doing there.

"I ain't got time to talk to you lady." He said dismissively, as he tried to walk past her without stopping. "I don't know what you put on me, but I'm good."

"I didn't put anything on you." The old woman replied. "I just opened your eyes."

"Opened my eyes? Lady get the hell on! I'm seeing another woman that I used to beat up, *fifteen years ago, face pop in the middle of having sex with my current woman." Lonnie snapped at her. He was pissed.*

"Listen, Lonnie." The old woman persisted. "It's getting heavy. That last spirit is upon you. You're seeing faces transition already?"

"Lady, I ain't got time." Lonnie brushed her off, storming away into the crowd.

"Yo, cuz? What's wrong?" Joe asked him as he saw him approaching. He caught Lonnie as he started to storm past him.

"I seen you talking to that older lady over there, looking like you was about to go off. What was she doing, hitting on you?" Joe asked him, laughing in Lonnie's face like it was one of the funniest moments ever.

"Naw.... man.." Lonnie shook his head. "I think she messing with my mind. I met her today at work, and the crazy freak started telling me about myself. And demons chasing me too, all kinds of B.S."

He turned and slapped some money onto the counter and signaled to the bartender.

"I need two shots of Patron, please."

Lonnie turned back towards Joe, feeling bugged out.

"Bro, she's staring at you right now from across the room." Joe said with humor. "She probably wants you."

"Stop playing Joe." Lonnie grumbled in irritation, as he took his second shot down. "Man, she brought up something...well allowed me to dig up something that I didn't want to remember."

"Remember what?" Said Joe.

"Man, I don't even want to go off into it, cuz." Lonnie evaded the question. "All I'm gonna say is...Cookie. I thought I could actually keep thoughts of her buried under the dirt. But I think this broad jumped into my head, and seen some hidden stuff that could really expose and destroy me."

"Well cuz, that's the past. And she can't possibly know everything, with her fine ole self." Joe remarked, staring at her from across the room.

"Did you not just hear me?" Lonnie said in annoyance. "She knows something, and she's been in my freaking head. Man, you know what I think? She's a witch."

Unhealthy soul Ties

- Not every fruit is designed to be eaten -

Chapter five

They both started laughing, taking some more shots of patron.

The very next morning, Lonnie woke up in his bed with a hangover. He contemplated if he wanted to go into work.

"Awwe ...damn...my head. I think I had too many shots." He said to himself, putting on his pants, yawning as he headed down the hallway, grabbed his keys and headed out the door.

'Good morning baby. How did you sleep?' Was the text that popped up from his phone from KeeKe.

He responded back.

'I slept pretty good. But a bit tired. I had a few drinks with my cousin Joe last night, after I left your house.'

Lonnie started up the car and pulled off, turning up his radio and listening to some of his old 90's music. R. Kelly's 'Your body's calling me' was playing, as he texted her on the way to work. He headed down the street, twenty minutes away, sipping on his coffee.

Just as he pulled into the parking lot, guess who he bumped into....the little old lady.

"Hey you, would you just talk to me?" The old woman sounded genuinely concerned today.

"Lady, not right now. I'm already five minutes late, and I don't need you making my head worse than it is." Lonnie responded quickly.

But she walked over closer to him, and whispered softly.

"What happened to the plug? What did you and Cookie do? Where is she now?"

Lonnie stopped in his tracks and stared at her for a long moment, swallowing nervously before replying.

"I don't know what you're talking about."

The old woman pressed him again.

"What did Cookie make you do? Where is she now?"

Lonnie continued to stare at her real deep, and then replied.

"I don't know where Cookie is, I haven't seen her in almost fifteen years. All I know, is that she had a son. And I found that out through friends, after she disappeared."

"You still haven't answered my question." The old lady wouldn't let it go. *"What happened to the plug? Her boyfriend?"*

Lonnie had enough.

"Lady, I gotta get in. This conversation is over." He started to walk away.

"You killed him." She blurted out.

"Look lady, I didn't kill nobody! And I would appreciate it if you would leave me the hell alone!" Lonnie shouted at her.

But the old woman ignored him.

"And Cookie got rid of the baby." As she smiled, she finally walked away, leaving him with those last chilling words.

Lonnie gave the woman another deep stare, disturbed in more ways than one.

"Alright." He called after her. *"We'll talk, but right now is not the time. And besides, you have no idea what you're talking about."*

By the afternoon during work, Lonnie was so stressed and deep in thought about what the old lady had revealed to him. He thoughts were taking a dark turn.

'Damn, I gotta find out all this woman knows about me, and possibly get rid of her.' He thought to himself.

"What you daydreaming about?"

It was a co-worker by the name of Cynthia he used to mess around with, before he started dating KeeKe.

"Nothing." Lonnie replied. "But you can tell the coordinator that I have to hit the bathroom, and could he watch my desk while I do that."

"Sure." Said Cynthia. "You a lil bit snappy today, you sure you don't want to talk about it?"

"I'm good." Lonnie said stoically.

Cynthia walked off to get the coordinator for him.

While in the bathroom, Lonnie threw some water on his face, while talking to himself in the mirror.

"This is crazy, this is crazy!" He repeated to himself over and over. He headed over to the stall

and shut the door, sitting on the toilet and pulling out his phone. But right before he logged into his messages, there was a knock on the door.

"I'm in here!" Lonnie shouted in annoyance.

Then a voice replied back.

"Don't you want to let me in?"

Lonnie frowned in confusion. "Cynthia?" He said.

"The voice started to laugh softly. "Nigga! Open the door and quit playin, cause I know you're not on the toilet, but on your phone."

Lonnie opened the door, and sure enough it was Cynthia.

"What do you want, Cynthia?" He snapped at her. "I just need some time to myself, can I get five minutes of that, Damn!"

"Five minutes is all you need? I got you." Cynthia replied.

Lonnie paused and looked at her. "Got what?" He asked her.

She dropped to her knees and grabbed his shaft, looking him in the eyes and said, "I got you. I know exactly what you need."

Lonnie didn't pull back, not for one second, as she slowly placed the tip of his wand in her mouth. As the spit ran down her chin, sucking his soul away.

Lonnie's thoughts were in a maze, wondering like, 'wow. I can't believe this is happening. Right here, and right now in the bathroom. Maybe this is what I needed.' He closed his eyes as he released into the jaws of life.

"My god." Lonnie softly cried out, as he pulled back from her thick lips, releasing his sensitive head, and watching her down every drip of life in her throat.

"You good." Cynthia said, as she got up off her knees, wiping her mouth. "That was a lot of stress built up within you." She smiled at him, and then walked out of the bathroom.

Lonnie didn't even have to wipe down, because she cleaned up pretty well. That's when he started to think to himself.

'Oh man, what did I just do? But oh well, that did kind of relieve me.' He pulled his pants up and headed out as well.

Meanwhile, back at home, KeeKe was sitting up with her coffee and her electronic cigarette, watching the x-files. She was in a very comfortable spot at the moment. Her baby was at the childcare center, so she had the day to herself.

'I guess I'll finish up this last load of laundry before I cook dinner.' She thought to herself, watching the end of x-files.

Walking around the house with her boy shorts on, and her cut off t-shirt with her hair wrapped up. Looking as sexy as any other black woman. Laid back, with hot class. Booty so round and firm, its like every step she took it shook as if it had a natural twerk.

This woman had a lot going for herself. Even though she grew up in foster homes, due to her parents not getting along. She turned out quite well for herself regardless the struggles that hit her.

However, KeeKe had been in a lot of abusive relationships, mentally and physically. But she'd managed to see her way out of them and into success.

She had her own, and even though she had a child, she held it down. The relationship between *her father and mother was unknown, due to she had her own life, and it felt right.*

*****

"Can you talk now, Mr. McGill?" Said the old lady, using Lonnie's last name for the first time. It still gave him the chills wondering how she knew so much about him. He had punched out of work, and was headed to the parking lot. He sighed as he turned towards her.

"Ok lady, we can talk. Meet me at the coffee house at 5:30."

"I'll meet you there." The old lady replied. "And by the way, there are better ways of relieving yourself than letting people suck on you during bathroom breaks." She gave him a knowing look.

Lonnie was already too through with the woman.

"Look lady, just meet me where I told you to be, and stay the hell out of my business, damn!" He hopped into his car, and turned on his music. Listening to H-town, knocking the boots. He shook his head as he drove off.

"This woman is trippin me the hell out." Lonnie said to himself. "This is crazy, damn. What she gonna do, watch me drive off too?" He muttered, as he saw her still standing there in the rearview, gazing after him, as he took off down the street.

Lonnie pulled a half blunt out of the ashtray, taking it to the head.

'I so need this before I meet with this witch.' He thought to himself.

He dials up KeeKe and puts her on speaker phone.

"Hey, hey! What you doing, I'm just getting off." He said to her.

"Nothing. Washing clothes and cooking dinner. You gonna fall through?" KeeKe replied.

"Oh yeah, as soon as I come back from this meeting I gotta go to in about an hour or two." Said Lonnie. "But I'm headed to my house for a split second."

"Ok. I'm cooking baked chicken and yams, with some hot water corn bread and greens, and mac and cheese. So I'll save you a plate."

"Cool." Lonnie replied, anticipating the meal. "That's what's up. Cooking for your man." They both laughed at that.

"But I'll catch up to you in a bit."

"Ok baby. Be safe." KeeKe hung up.

Waiting at the stop light, Lonnie noticed another woman in the parking lot putting her groceries into the trunk of her car.

Oooweee...he started to get this itch where he'd been scratching at for the past few weeks. The woman that he noticed had a nice figure. Apple bottom jeans with a betty boop T-shirt. With some really thick corn rolls going to the back of her head.

He pulled up on her so close, she yelled out at him.

"Damn, dude! You goin mess around and side swipe my car!"

"I got you baby...I mean Miss..." Lonnie corrected his grammar. "I seen you putting your groceries in and just thought I'd help a pretty lady."

The conversation

- Be mindful of the company you keep -

Chapter Six

"Well I don't need no help." Said the woman. But Lonnie got out anyway and began to start placing some of the groceries into her trunk and backseat.

"What you want?" The woman asked him.

"I don't want nothing but a little conversation with a pretty woman." Lonnie replied smoothly.

"But what if I told you I have a man?"

"Then I can respect that." Lonnie said. "Then I'll walk away, and tell you have a good day."

"Hmmm...well guess what? I have a man."

Lonnie squinted his eyes, like yeah right, and she started smiling.

"So I see you like to play." Lonnie smiled back. "By the way, I'm L, but people call me Lonnie."

"Well Mr. Lonnie, I do have a man, well somewhat, but I appreciate you helping me out with my groceries." The woman responded.

"No problem." Said Lonnie. "Well can I leave my number with you?"

"Didn't I just tell you that I have a man?" She replied.

"Well I offered you my number just in case he wasn't there to vent, chill, hang out or whatever. Ain't nothing wrong with being friends, right?"

"Friends? Boy you didn't even ask me my name." The woman chuckled.

"Well I figured you'd offer it since I told you mine." Lonnie came back at her with a confidence.

She smiled and replied to him.

"Belinda...that's my name. But you can call me Linda."

"Well Linda," Lonnie responded, "that's a good start to a friendship."

And they shook hands. Lonnie looked her up and down as she smiled.

"What you lookin at?" Said Linda.

Lonnie chuckled. "I just like what I see." He remarked.

"Do you?" Linda began to slightly flirt back. "I gotta go, Mr. Lonnie. And I guess I'll give you a call sometime this week if my man approves of it." And she walked off.

"Make sure you tell him that I was checking you out, and that you was being real good, and not a bad girl." Lonnie said as she was leaving.

"Whateva!" Linda laughed as they both got into their cars and drove off.

Lonnie headed home to change his clothes. Knowing he had to head back to the coffee house to meet up with the old woman. She knew so much about his secret personal life. He headed back on the road, to the coffee shop, and eventually pulled up.

Soon as he came into the shop, the old woman waved him down.

"Hey, I can't be too long. I didn't eat yet." Lonnie told her.

"Well, do you want to order a little something?" The old woman replied.

"No thanks." Lonnie shook his head. *"I got something waiting for me when I get back home."*

"Ok, ok...you smell pretty good. It smells like Joop cologne." The woman said, eyeing him.

Lonnie grew a bit uncomfortable at her staring.

"Yes, it is. So what's going on? Tell me what you think you know…"

The woman looked at him for a moment longer and then smiled, raising her head slowly, as she began to speak.

"Succubus haunts you. It's a spirit. The spirit of seduction and lust. Everything that it takes interest in, it wants to taste."

"What do you mean, taste?" Lonnie questioned her.

"It has a need, a want, it craves the flesh. The orgasms, the manipulations…" The old woman insisted.

But Lonnie was still looking confused.

"Look lady, you're gonna have to fill me in on more than what you're talking about." Lonnie grunted in frustration.

"You're tied to whatever it was that Cookie put on you. It latched itself onto you, which explains why you keep things hidden away and stored."

The woman further shared with him.

"It's haunting your conscious, and sex to you is like a crave. A blunt, like crack or heroine. Anything that looks good to you, you want to sleep with it. But in reality, it isn't you. You'll begin to see things. Shadows to illustrations. This woman has hexed you. In other words...cursed you."

"How did she curse me? By putting a spell on me, or what?" Lonnie still didn't believe what she was saying.

"Possibly in your food, drops of blood, certain orbs seasoning, or even sand salts." The woman replied.

"This woman has tied herself to you to the point she doesn't want to lose connection."

She stared at him quietly, before continuing.

"So tell me what happened. I can help you break this tie that haunts you, Lonnie. Tell me what is it that you two hold in secret together."

"I don't really want to go into detail with what happened." Said Lonnie. He started to drift off a bit, before he went into his mode, telling the story.

"Cookie was quite controlling. Julian found out we were messing around. But to make a long story short, we set him up into catching us."

"Set him up how?" The woman asked.

"We got him to come over to the house. Well basically, to come to her place while I was still there." Said Lonnie.

"So you killed him there at his own house?"

"Look, I don't know what came over me." Lonnie shrugged. "All I know is that when he walked in, and began to talk to her for a moment, I stayed hidden behind the door in the kitchen with a hammer in my hand. And just when she led him into the kitchen, and I was about to knock him out, I caught eye contact with him, and he paused. And next thing you know, Cookie hits him with a jar of baby food, clutched in her fist.

It dazed him, but didn't knock him out. So I hit him twice in the chest with the hammer, it nearly broke the bones in his chest, as the blood gushed out of his mouth. Then Cookie whispered something to me as she watched Julian gasping for air...."

Lonnie remembered her chilling words as if she had said them only moments ago...

***

Succubus

- When the soul is poisoned, the heart will never know it -

Chapter Seven

"We gotta kill him." Cookie whispered it like a pledge, watching him steadily.

Lonnie looked at her in shock. "No, we can't." He disagreed.

"Nigga he's going to kill us if he survives." Cookie replied angrily. Then stormed off.

Lonnie paced the floor, flipping out like, damn this chick is crazy! Then suddenly he heard it.

Bat! Bat! Bat!

Cookie shot off three rounds into Julian's body. Two in the head, one in the chest.

"What the...!!" Lonnie shouted in surprise.

Cookie smiled and walked over to Lonnie, and kissed him. She whispered to him again.

"It had to be done." She dropped the gun. "I know a place we can hide the body."

***

Now, as Lonnie came back to the present, he saw the old woman staring at him calmly.

"Wow. So where did you take the body?" The woman asked him.

"We wrapped him up in an old rug and duct taped it. Then buried him by the railroad tracks." Lonnie replied. "Some dogs found the remains and it was dug up. His murder is an unsolved mystery. They stopped searching for his killer a month after people realized there was no trace in finding who did it."

"So what happened with Cookie?" The woman asked him.

"Weeks later, she disappeared. But every now and then, I dream of her. Or have some type of vision of her." Lonnie answered.

"Wow." The old lady exclaimed. "So she visits you through vision and dreams?"

"Yes." Lonnie said in resignation. "Yes, she does."

***

Lonnie continued to talk with the old woman. Discussing everything with her concerning Cookie. Because it was more to it than she could imagine. And Lonnie wanted her to know the truth.

"It was like Cookie would come see me in these dreams, and the murder scene would replay all over. But at the same time, before or after it began, she would make love to me."

"Make love to you? In what way?" The woman questioned him.

"It was like I couldn't move." Lonnie answered her. "She would paralyze me and drain me dry. Sucking the soul out of my body. I couldn't take it. I couldn't even breathe during intercourse." He shook his head.

"I would wake up with her on top of me, giving me the ride of my life. I fall into her with no ease, and she would bounce to the point I would explode. Then I would wake up."

"Can I tell you something, Lonnie?" The old woman asked him.

"Yeah."

"It was succubus. She's been making love to you for years." The old woman said, in a grave tone. "In other words, Cookie has never left you. Her spirit has followed you everywhere. You've attracted several women without even trying to. Slept with several women on first nights. You have an addiction. That juice box has got you trapped. There's something about the woman you're with now."

The old woman peered at him intensely.

"You must watch her closely."

Lonnie began to think about KeeKe, and how innocent she was. But at the same time, he thought it strange how she seemed to fall in love rather quickly. But then again, she hadn't used the three letter word yet. But it was her actions that showed how she felt about him.

He walked out of the coffee shop, his mind just cluttered, thinking heavier than he ever had before. He headed over to KeeKe's house for some dinner.

On his way there, Lonnie began to see flashbacks on every woman that he'd ever touched. Whether it was intercourse or oral. And there were many.

Tameka, Lashawn, Tammy, Shontell, Nicole, Nikki, Lachele. He'd slept with all these women several times within the past three months. And a few more while he was with KeeKe.

He pulled up finally to her house a little bit after seven pm, and knocked on the door. KeeKe answered it right away.

"What's up baby, I've been waiting on you. How was your meeting?" KeeKe asked, greeting him with a kiss.

"It was ok. Same o, same o." Lonnie replied with a smile.

"Ok cool. I have your food already warmed up, it's in the oven. You can go get your plate while I head to this basement to fold the rest of the clothes, it was a lot." KeeKe rushed off to handle her laundry.

Lonnie sat down and ate his food, while KeeKe was in the basement handling her clothes. But soon after he was finished, he headed down there to check on her and see what was taking her so long.

"Key, you almost finished? Do you need some help?" He called out as he entered the basement.

"No baby, I got this." KeeKe replied. But Lonnie crept down the stairs anyway. He saw her squatted over, pulling the clothes out of the dryer.

"Oowee..." He whispered, as he crept upon her from behind to bump his shaft against her thick soft heaven.

"This is sexy, love." Lonnie said to her, moving into her cushiony warmth.

"I can already see you're not going to let me finish these clothes." KeeKe replied with a chuckle.

But Lonnie pulled back.

"You can finish, I won't touch you. I'm a head back upstairs and wait on you."

"Wait on me?" KeeKe sounded surprised. "Ok, you do that."

Lonnie went back upstairs while KeeKe finished folding her laundry.

Ten minutes went by, and Lonnie was undressed with pretty much everything off, except his boxers. Then he heard KeeKe call him from downstairs.

"Hey L, can you give me a hand with these baskets?"

So he headed back downstairs intending to help with the baskets, and saw KeeKe on top of the dryer completely naked, biting her lip.

"Come and get me." She said softly.

Lonnie didn't hesitate.

He walked over to her and picked her up as she wrapped her legs around his waist. She said to him...

"Let me hold it, and put it in."

As she slipped his hard brick muscle off into her milky way, he pounded her senseless.

Lonnie picked her up even higher, to the point both of her legs were on his shoulders, while he was tasting her center of sweetness. Then onto the dryer, digging deep down off into her puddle of honey. Brick glazed with her cream, flooded all over his navel.

He took her to the table, as he inflicted her with a deeper grind, while she sucked on his fingers. He gripped her neck from the back while pulling her hair, as he continued to feed her.

The sex was intense, the drive made no sense, the look in her eyes were like a fire in a blaze...oh...my....it was love that would make you want to die. She was like an overflow fountain filled with tears, with no time to pass by.

His shaft was like a laced blunt that she would hit and choke soft, his high took her into another galaxy, that milked her milky way at take off.

Then suddenly, Lonnie looked down during her second climax, just as it began to emerge, and saw Cookie's face.

"What the hell?!" He pulled back instantly, shaken and confused.

KeeKe looked at him with a peculiar distinguished expression on her face. As if she knew what was going on.

"What is it?" She asked him sweetly.

Lonnie looked at her, and she smiled at him. It was KeeKe's face again. Not Cookie's.

"I don't feel right." Lonnie replied, still disturbed by what he'd seen.

"How do you feel?" KeeKe asked him innocently.

He began to see doubles of her face, the image melding and separating. At the same time, seeing Cookie's face once again.

"Don't you love me, Lonnie?" KeeKe asked softly.

Lonnie felt as if he was going out of his mind. He was hallucinating, looking all around, panicking, while KeeKe began to laugh at him.

"I must got that good...good." She said smugly.

"What in the hell did you do to me?!" Lonnie shouted, as he stumbled over to the stairs, trying to walk away.

"I didn't do anything." Said KeeKe. "All I gave you was a little bit of this juice box."

Lonnie passed out on the stairs.

***

The Soul sucking

- What controls your mind, can destroy your life -

Chapter Eight

Moments later, he woke up strapped to the bed. His legs, arms, waist and side, were all pinned to the bed. He was blind folded.

"What the hell?!" Lonnie cried out in shock.

KeeKe crawls over to him and got on top of him.

"Shhh..keep it down. I don't want you to wake up the baby." She whispered in his ear.

"KeeKe what's going on? Why am I blindfolded and chained to this bed?" Lonnie shot back at her.

But KeeKe didn't answer him right away. She started kissing him on his neck and chest. Then she finally responded.

"Let me go get something to cool you off, because baby, you're hot right now."

"Cool me off? Cool me off with what?" Lonnie asked, his tension rising through the roof.

KeeKe got up and headed to the kitchen, grabbing a knife and placing it on the stove to heat up the blade. The blade became so hot, that it was orange now. KeeKe then grabbed an ice cube, and returned to the room. And got back on top of him.

"I'm back, baby. Tell me do you like this?" She said to him.

KeeKe took the knife and started touching the ice cubes, while dripping the water from the cubes onto his chest.

"You like?" She asked him.

"What am I supposed to like about it?" Lonnie responded gruffly, while he was still blindfolded and tied up.

In reply, KeeKe took the hot blade and started using it across his chest, spelling out a name.

Lonnie began to scream in pain.

"Why are you doing this to me?!!" He shouted out at her. The pain was unbelievable. KeeKe started laughing, then suddenly snatched the blindfold off of him.

"Nigga! Did you just ask me why?" KeeKe laughed again, as she started licking his face from the chin up to his forehead.

Suddenly, her face began to transition in front of him. As he started seeing illusions again. KeeKe grabbed his chin, looking him in the eyes.

"Who do you see, tell me!" She ordered him to answer her.

"I see an old face!" Lonnie cried out helplessly. "What did you do to me?"

Lonnie knew something was not right, and that KeeKe must have drugged him. She had placed something into his food.

He finally looked down at his chest, and noticed the carvings that she made in his skin. There was a name written on his flesh.

It said: Cookie.

Lonnie's eyes bucked in shock.

"What! Why would you carve her name into my chest?!" He couldn't believe it.

"Isn't that who you've been seeing?" KeeKe asked him sweetly. "Open your eyes wider and see reality."

"How realer can it possibly get? Please let me go. Untie me!" Lonnie struggled against the bonds.

"Untie you? Now you want me to let you go?" KeeKe said smoothly. "I've been tied to you for years. How you gonna ask to break free from me now? Don't you love me? Don't I make you feel good?" Her smile was frozen in place.

"I've changed everything about you. From your walk, your talk, and even your emotions."

Lonnie began to cry out, his rage at the situation was palpable. He finally looked at KeeKe and asked her.

"What the hell does carving Cookie's name in my chest have to do with all this?"

KeeKe smiled at him.

As she was smiling, while still on top of him, her face started to transition into something that was mouth dropping. Lonnie grew speechless at what he was witnessing.

"Are you shocked? I told you I was latched onto you forever. I've been watching you the whole time."

"This can't be..." Lonnie stammered in shock.

It was the old woman. It was her the whole time.

"I knew you were a witch." Lonnie spoke in fear, staring at her.

The old woman laughed at him, and replied back, smugly.

"You're a fool. Look a little bit closer. Have I been with you so long, that you can't recognize me?"

"Lady, I don't know you." Lonnie said angrily now.

"But you've slept with me several times. Even helped me at the grocery store and put my bags away for me. You even helped me get rid of a dead body and dispose of it near Wicks Park, buried beneath the railroad tracks..." The woman said calmly, and with great satisfaction.

"What?!" Lonnie's head was trying to wrap around what she'd just said. He started to think about it.

"So all these people that I was in contact with, was you?" He asked in disbelief.

"Lonnie baby, I never left you." The old woman replied.

"Never left me...I never knew you. I don't know you, you don't know me."

The old woman cut his legs loose, but kept the knife up to his throat. She leaned closer and whispered to him...

"I'm Cookie."

It was as if Lonnie was only waiting for confirmation.

"That explains it all." He muttered. "You knew too much, and I never spoke of the park near the tracks we dumped the body at."

"Smart...very smart." The old woman said with a smile.

"It's been some years baby, since we seen one another. And I gotta hand it to you. I taught you very well. You done became a freak. It's just too bad I could never trust you, given the fact you cheated on me, with me, several times."

Lonnie started to shudder.

"Cookie, really? I did nothing to you to deserve all of this."

The old woman shook her head slowly, and smiled.

"I'm not Cookie. That's just one of the bodies I used. But you can call me, Succubus, if you like. Or, *if it makes you feel any better, you can stick with Cookie. I have many names. But Succubus is my real name."*

The old woman began to walk around the room, transitioning into all the women that Lonnie had slept with, right in front of his face. It was like she was a shape shifter in a scifi movie.

She began to speak to him as she changed and shifted.

"All these people you see before you, are in you, Lonnie. Oh my god, you slept with a lot of people. Ask yourself this, Lonnie." She paused and looked at him. "How many knots do you think are tied off into you?"

She then released his arms just by staring at him, as she walked around the room. Changing into all the different souls that were latched onto him.

"You have all these spirits on you, but I am your favorite, which is lust." Said Succubus.

"Did you see how easy it was for me to give you oral sex at work?"

Lonnie stood up and faced her.

"What do you want from me?" He asked her.

"I already have you." She replied with a chuckle.

He decided to try a different tactic.

"What happened to you being pregnant? He questioned.

"I was never pregnant." Said Succubus. "It was you that was impregnated. I planted a seed in you. Each time you slept with me, I placed something within you, that caused you to go to the next, and then the next, and so forth. Our baby is your addiction. You are addicted to the juice box."

She turned towards him and he saw a glimpse of who she really was, the voluptuous beauty was irresistible.

"I inflicted this gift in you, and now you want to get rid of me?! After all the beautiful moods I've given you! Didn't I take away all your stress when you needed it?"

All the time she was explaining all the goods she had given him, she continued to shift into the women he'd slept with.

As Lonnie was putting his boxer shorts back on, his mindset was fixed and planning on running out of the house, the first opportunity he got.

Drowning in lust

- The most beautiful rose, is still surrounded by thorns -

Chapter Nine

As soon as it was clear, Lonnie jetted out of the house. But it was too easy. She didn't even put up a fight. She chased him out the door, then just paused, and smiled.

"He has no idea that he can never run far..." Succubus said to herself, as she watched him go. "No matter where he goes, I will always be with him. I am inside of him."

Lonnie flagged a car down, after many of them had passed him by. One finally stopped for him.

"Can I get dropped off on Beechwood please." Lonnie asked the driver.

"Sure, hop in, what's going on?"

The driver noted his panicked expression, as Lonnie jumped in the car as if he was running for his life.

"She's a freaking witch! Yo, you don't wanna know, just go!"

Lonnie instructed the driver to take off, as he tried to control his racing heart. He was breathing hard as ever, as they took off down the street. Pushing 80 mph in a Volkswagen.

Finally reaching his destination, he headed into his home. Jumping on the phone, he called up Joe to come over. When his cousin arrived, he tried to explain what he'd been through.

"Cuz, you won't believe this mess! Cookie is here."

"What you mean?" Joe replied.

"That old lady, and all the women I've encountered with, were all her! This hoe's a witch!" Lonnie could barely contain his hysteria.

Joe sighed and responded calmly.

"Bro, you buggin. She got that good, good that she dropped on you."

"Cuz, all jokes aside." Lonnie said, desperate to make him understand. "She's a witch."

Suddenly there was a knock on the door.

Lonnie felt an instant chill of apprehension, when he heard it. "Nigga, don't go answer it." He warned his cousin.

"Cuz calm down, I got you. That booty must be like good weed." Joe laughed, as he walked towards the door to answer it.

When Joe got to the door, he opened it up and looked outside. But no one was there.

"What the..."

Joe mumbled to himself in confusion.

"Cuz, ain't no one here." He said, staring into the empty walkway.

"Cuz, I told you..." Lonnie replied to him as he joined him, but still felt his nerves shaking. They both looked around, and went inside and checked all the windows.

Suddenly Lonnie felt a pinch on his backside.

"Bro, quit playing!" Lonnie was pissed at his cousin. But then a voice responded in a whisper...

"I like the way you move that ass."

Lonnie turned around swiftly, and stood face to face with Cookie.

Without hesitation, he grabbed her by the neck and started to choke her like crazy. All the while she had the biggest smile on her face. He loosened up his grip a bit, as she gasped for breath.

"Lonnie, you don't really want to hurt me." Cookie said seductively. "You want to love me." Her face began to shift into many other women from the past.

"These are all the souls you are tied to. You are a part of all of us."

Lonnie's face scrunched up in rage.

"No!" He yelled out furiously.

Meanwhile, Joe was hidden out of sight to the side, witnessing everything.

Cookie suddenly blew into Lonnie's face, and instantly he went numb, his body going stiff as a board.

"Didn't I tell you that you could never part from me?" Cookie said softly to him. "Breathe...breathe..."

It was what she would always say to him, as she sat on his chest during love making, and his dreams.

"It's kind of hard to breathe, isn't it Lonnie? Especially when a witch is sitting on your chest?" She chuckled as he struggled with his air.

What many didn't understand was that Cookie herself was cursed and hurt. She'd had so many sexual partners and was raped at an early age, by her mother's boyfriend. She didn't know how to love.

However, in dealing with her heartbreak, she'd gotten involved with witchcraft, and fought through her pain with dark magic. She would destroy her ex-lovers by poisoning their minds. Confusing them, and caused some to even kill themselves. She manipulated and controlled them all, to the point where each of them went crazy and chose death.

"Cookie...I loved you. Why are you doing this to me?" Lonnie said quietly, looking at her steadily.

"Nigga, you love me? No you don't. You love what I do, and how I make you feel. You don't love me." Cookie replied bitterly.

Lonnie was struggling to breathe, because Cookie was still sitting on his chest, draining him.

"How you going to tell me I don't love you? After all I've done for you?" Lonnie questioned her.

"Don't you mean after all I've done for you?" Cookie remarked. "I sucked the soul out of your

body. Made you feel like somebody. When you were lonely, I relieved you, and received you. I was every woman you've ever slept with. I covered you."

"What do you mean every woman I've ever slept with?" Lonnie asked, needing to buy time.

"I was Katrina. Tasha, Pammy and Dina, Sharon, Bri. All these women that tied to you. I was Pammy when she deceived you, that caused you to drift into what you are now." Cookie stared at him, as she told his story.

"Your heart was with Pammy and Dina, not me." Her eyes took on a gleam.

"Didn't you see me in Pammy that day, the second she left you and walked out your door? Didn't you see me when Dina told you on the toilet, she wanted you, and the nigga she was cheating on you with at the same time, before you decided no more?"

The flashbacks came at Lonnie once again in that moment, remembering the faces of both women Cookie brought up.

Both situations were very similar. Then the faces began to shift. Same eyes, same smile, same motives, same understanding, same spirit.

"Now tell me, Lonnie..." Cookie said softly. "Who gives better sex. Them, or me? But wait, hold up...they all were me!" She began to laugh at him.

Joe crept out of the house through a window and ran to seek help. Because now he realized that woman was more than just crazy, and just might kill Lonnie.

He took off the moment he left the premises, and headed over to one of their friend's house to use a cell phone.

"Hello, 911? I need some assistance at 149 Vestrie Drive. My cousin is about to lose his life." Joe spoke hurriedly to the dispatcher.

The emergency dispatcher took his information and said they would head over there. But Joe knew the police. They were in the hood, a place where there was always violence. So they would take their time getting to him.

Meanwhile, back at the house, Lonnie was getting sucked in, and drowning in lust. Cookie pretty much had him under water, buried deep within her core.

"You'll forever remember me. Your soul belongs to us. You can't resist." Cookie said in satisfaction.

Lonnie was so zoned out, while she took control of him. Every suck, touch, kiss, nibble, was drowning every bit of his soul.

"Touch it," She whispered, "grab all of me. Taste my pleasures. This sweet honey bee. Tell me you love, and are willing to inhale all of me."

Then Lonnie whispered back to her...

"I want you...I need you...I yearn you...I bleed you..."

He was now in a deeper trance. Her soul was now connected even further into his own. To the point his face began to shift. Cookie whispered in his ear, the very second he began to reach orgasm.

"Your soul is mine." She said in ecstasy, and inhaled him deeply.

The road of Redemption

- In order to kill a snake, you must first recognize that it is a snake -

Chapter Ten

Cookie's eyes rolled up into the back of her head, and she looked up and smiled, laughing. Then she looked down at him, while still on top of him, and collapsed onto his chest.

Lonnie began to scream

"Help! Somebody help me!" But no one could hear him.

He cried out as Cookie's body lay lifeless on top of him, as he laid underneath her, drained and weak.

She was drooling at the mouth, with her eyes rolled to the back of her head. She was most definitely dead, getting cold as ice, as she lay on top of him.

Suddenly there was a beating at the door, and a shout. "Police! Open up!"

"Lonnie screamed out to them.

"I can't move! I'm in here, help me, she's dead and there's no one else in here."

The police broke down the door. Two cops came running into the house with their guns drawn, finding nothing but Cookie butt naked on top of Lonnie, lifeless.

"Help me." Lonnie pleaded with them.

The police stood there stunned, seeing a man held hostage somewhat, by a naked woman in bed.

It almost looked as if she'd had a heart attack during sex.

The police called for an ambulance, and Joe came running in right along side them.

"Cuz, you alright?" Joe asked him worriedly.

Lonnie looked at him in annoyance.

"Nigga, you left me. You left me up in this piece with this crazy freak out broad!" He was pissed at him.

"Who you think called the police, dummy?" Joe replied.

"I know cuz, you looked out. But you still left me, nigga." Lonnie came back at him, then they both laughed at the craziness of the situation.

He paused before they shut the doors of the ambulance.

"Give me a second." Lonnie asked the paramedics, before they closed the doors. He wanted to see them carry Cookie's body out in the body bag. Cracking a smile and feeling relieved when he saw it.

Joe looked at Lonnie and said...

"Better her than you, right?"

Lonnie nodded his head in agreement. "Damn...but you're right. Better her than me."

Then the ambulance closed the doors and pulled off, taking Lonnie to the hospital. While Cookie's body went the other way, headed to the morgue.

Shortly later in the hospital, while being checked out, Lonnie was laying in the bed. He was beginning to think about all the things that had happened to him, and the stuff that was brought up, that he thought was buried. Not knowing that all the while, it never really left. And his past had slept under him the whole time.

'Wow.' He thought to himself. 'I was in love with a dark illusion. Something that brought me into confusion and disruption. It nearly controlled my life. Someone that I thought had some potential of being my wife. But all she was, was a 200 pump.

That made me sweat. Moans and groans that kept the sheets wet.

She blotted my vision, and became my addiction. Made love to me endlessly from the rooftop to the kitchen. I sold my soul, to a control so bold. And lost my identity to a monster that unfolds.

My heart is so cold, all I can think about now is smoking bolds, and aftermodes, and bank roles, and catching hoes.

Should I let this change me for the good, or say screw it, and rock out for the hood. Yeah, it was Karma that I rep. She snatched my heart, and sucked the soul nearly out my chest.

I confess, lord yes. She had me gone off those Carmel thighs and delicious breasts. Her taste was like no other, a fruit so sweet that it must of fell from heaven.

This damn demon that latched itself onto me, and now I can't sleep at night, due to its mentally and spiritually raping me.

Succubus...I was sleeping with the enemy.'

Lonnie's thoughts drifted off, as he closed his eyes and rested on the pillow.

Juice Box

***

Back at the morgue, laying on the table for examinations, was Cookie's body. Peacefully laying with her eyes rolled in the back of her head.

"What a pretty lady" The mortician remarked as he looked at her.

"We see a lot of these type of women come and go. I wonder what we'll find in you, and your cause of death." He said in anticipation of searching her.

As he took a warm wash cloth and began to wipe down her naked body, the phone rang. He stepped away for only a moment to answer it.

But when he picked it up, he noticed a soft chuckle on the other line. It sounded distant and fading.

"Hello....hello?" He spoke into the phone, confused. But no one answered. So he shrugged it off and hung up.

As he turned around, he came face to face with Cookie. She was standing in front of him, naked and smiling.

Just as the mortician was about to scream, his mouth open in shock, she inhaled him in, with a deep breath. Sucking the air out of his mouth.

He went instantly mute. And began to feel as if he was suffocating. The man fell to the ground, and Cookie climbed on top of him. Speaking softly into his ear while chuckling.

"I know you, and know you very well. You fantasize about me...desire me." She stuck her tongue down in his ear.

"Oh yeeeeeees! I know something about you that no one knows."

The mortician began to shake and could not reply. She smiled at him and chuckled again.

"You like to play around with little girls." Cookie said smoothly.

But the mortician shook his head in denial, his eyes going wide. You could see the tears in his eyes, not knowing Cookie could see his soul.

Then Cookie spoke again...

"Shhh...you don't have to mess with little bitty girls anymore. Oh yeah...and dead bodies. You can *have a taste of this juice box. Feel this, and tell me if you like it."*

Cookie giggled...

Finally the mortician could speak. He stammered out a reply.

"Oh god, who are you?"

Cookie smiled at him and responded smoothly.

"God has nothing to do with this. But I have many names. My close friends call me Cookie. And some call me KeeKe. But dealing with you, hhmmm...I think I'd rather you call me Pammy for now. But as for my real name...

I am Succubus."

Epilogue

Lonnie came back to the present day, his story hitting the ears of many, as he ministered and shared his testimony.

"What a lot of people fail to understand, is that there's a lot of things that comes along with that pleasure. Many are more concerned about S.T.D.'s and using as much protection as they can.

However, there's nothing you can do to cover up your soul, to protect you from any demons, by having sexual encounters with them. We never know what people may have attached to them. Just because they look good on the outside, they may possibly be hiding something that contaminated them on the inside.

People pick up these unfamiliar spirits by having many sexual partners. And also picking up things from what they watch and listen to.

These demons such as Succubus, and Incubus, are spirits that attack the male and female, while they lay defenseless. The effects they send off makes you feel drained, weak and short of breath. As if you are suffocating.

Many call it sleep paralysis. In reality, it is a sex demon trying to take over you. It's basically having its way with you.

To avoid these types of demons, you have to be very careful with what you allow yourself to feed on.

The music you listen to, conversations you indulge in. As well as what you watch on television. TV shows, movies, etc.

However, we can't help what pops up on TV sometimes, these days. Just don't become addicted to it. Or feed yourself too much of it.

Let and allow the word of God to mold you, rather than a lyric or movie to control you."

Lonnie paused, finally feeling free from the burdens of his past. He finished off his testimony with a heart full of peace.

"Live your life on good measures. Don't sell your soul for the pleasures of this world. Because everything that is here now, that we see and touch....

is nothing but an illusion."

If you enjoyed *Juice Box*, then stay tuned for the final and climactic showdown.

The erotic battle between love and lust isn't quite over yet.

Find out what happens next in:

Juice Box 2
Lustfully consumed: The final betrayal

Turn the page for a nail-biting exclusive preview of *Juice Box 2,* coming soon!

Juice Box 2

Lustfully Consumed: The final betrayal

RICKY BOONE

Waking up the following day in his boxers, Lonnie slipped out of bed and into his house shoes, headed downstairs for his morning coffee.

"Damn, I gotta get this railing fixed before I break my neck." He thought to himself, as he made his way down the stairs.

"Juice box......"

Lonnie heard a sudden whisper within the silence, and he looked around quickly.

"I gots to be trippin." He muttered to himself.

Then he heard a giggle. Small giggles, consistent but faded, as if it were close but hidden away.

"Who's there?" Lonnie spoke into the room. But there was no answer. Just an uncomfortable silence remained.

"Yeah, I'm definitely trippin." Lonnie said gruffly, dismissing the weird moment, as he poured his coffee and sat at the kitchen table.

The sound of giggles started up again in the creepiest tone. But this time, there was a whisper.

"Shhh…. juice box…juice box…."

Lonnie ignored the sound. He believed he was just exhausted, and his mind was playing tricks on him. He wasn't the same man he used to be, almost a year ago. He had put many things behind him. Grown stronger. So he'd blocked out many things that he still felt often haunted him. But this time, it seemed stronger than ever…and he wondered why.

Heading up the stairs to his room and into the bathroom, Lonnie threw some water on his face. He ran the faucet as he looked at his reflection in the mirror.

Looking down at his hands, he filled them with more water and threw it once again over his face. But as he opened his eyes and stared at his image, it wasn't his reflection he saw.

It was Cookie's.

Her image stared back at him and smiled sweetly.

"I'm still here." She said softly. "Whether you accept it or not. I'm still here."

Ignoring the illusion, Lonnie splashed more water on his face, this time a bit faster.

Thinking a bit unsteadily to himself.

'I gotta get more sleep, or leave them pills alone.'

Lonnie was currently taking medication, that his doctor had told him would help with some of the trauma and depression he had been through. But he'd also told him that there may be side effects. And possibly hallucinations.

Flashbacks on all the sex he'd had with so many women over the years still haunted him. There were many issues and demons Lonnie still fought with. Especially in his dreams. Sleeping at night was the worst.

A lot of his friends had fell away from him due to the situation that had occurred. But they'd also seen that he had changed a lot in his life.

He was introduced to a whole new different set of friends. They were in the church, and were a complete change of environment that Lonnie needed in his life.

Jersey was an old friend who would come over and check on him every now and then. She was one of the very few who still remained with him. She understood him, and was the one who had encouraged him to slow down and take his time. To rethink things before he acted them out.

It was Jersey who now showed up at his house, to see how he was doing.

"Hey...hey...hello...?" Jersey welcomed herself into the house, since Lonnie had given her a key. It was her back up in case he didn't answer his phone when she called him. Which happened whenever he got caught up.

"I'm in the room, Jersey." Lonnie called out to her, when he heard her voice.

"What's good? I gotta little caught up in writing this sermon I was doing. So if that was you who called me, that explains why I didn't answer." He said to her as she entered the room.

"Yeah, you had me worried." Said Jersey. "I thought I was gonna walk up in here to your dead body." She chuckled, staring at him.

Lonnie laughed, finally looking up from his work, and seeing her standing by his desk.

"You can't be serious." He responded with a grin.

"I don't know. You meet some strange people. Especially that Cookie chick. And she used to have the creepiest laugh that gave me the chills." Jersey shook her head, remembering the one that had traumatized her friend.

"Well it was weird. But I had thought the giggle was cute at the time." Lonnie shrugged in response.

"Cute!" Jersey exclaimed in shock. "Whatever. Well I was just poppin in on you, to check on you. Especially since you need it, if you think the woman that tried to kill you had a cute laugh." She shook her head again.

"But seriously, you need to be a bit careful with this new chick you're seeing." Jersey's tone changed as she gave the subtle warning.

"You mean Erica?" Lonnie asked her in surprise.

"Yes." Jersey replied quickly.

But Lonnie waved his hand at her concerns, and smiled.

"She's saved and sanctified, and she's nowhere near crazy. She just wants a real good man." He defended Erica. "And I just might be that run up guy."

Jersey looked at him quietly for a moment, before responding.

"I was just saying be careful, ok?"

Not saying anything else, she headed out of the room, and left the house. Her thoughts for her longtime friend were in a turmoil.

Lonnie stared after her for a brief pause, and then shrugged it off and went back to focusing on his sermon. He was going over his notes, preparing for what he was going to teach that week.

But the medication he was taking had started to kick in even more, and he began seeing things. He fought it off, and rebuked the visions, as Cookie's face appeared within his mind again.

Her image was locked into his soul. A trauma that not even the medication could keep away.

Cookie's image would speak and whisper into his ear. As it was doing now.

"You can't get enough of me....I ain't going nowhere..." The giggles started up again, the grating sound he had once thought was so cute. They surrounded the room, causing him to feel paranoid every time he zoned out.

Lonnie jumped up from the desk and immediately got Erica on the phone. He needed her to take his mind off of things. To redirect his thoughts.

Later on, Lonnie headed over to a few members' house, to pray for some folks that were in need.

However, there was one in particular member of the church who knew of Lonnie's history and condition. He stayed up the street from him, and was a frequent visitor of the church.

His name was Paul Mackey. He was a youth director at a juvenile facility for teens, who attended services every now and then.

Paul kept his distance because he always thought dealing with Lonnie was a bit weird. But there was more to his reaction than he was admitting.

Paul had seen things surrounding Lonnie, and knew at times that he wasn't in the right frame of mind to be preaching. He knew the things he was dealing with, and the demons that were still surrounding him. So unknown to Lonnie, Paul would watch his house. Surveying on those that were coming and going. He would watch, and pray.

Because Paul knew, unlike Lonnie, he had a gift at seeing the truth.......

Stay tuned for

Juice Box 2

Lustfully Consumed: The final betrayal

Coming Soon!

LOOK OUT FOR THESE TITLES FROM AUTHOR RICKY BOONE AS WELL

THE DERANGED

PILLOW TALK 2

COMING SOON!

Visit the publishing website for more information

www.Ajbpublishing.com

About The Author

Born in Saginaw Michigan but raised in Grand Rapids Michigan, Ricky Boone discovered his passion for writing when he was 14 years old. He attempted to write his first book based on his love for movies.

"I've always seen part two and three even before they were created. However, I watched a movie called 'Under the Cherry Moon' by Prince, and the poetry he wrote in the movie inspired me, and I've been hooked ever since."

Author Ricky Boone links into many poets such as Desiree Renea, a poet that was dedicated into ministry in the church. She introduced him, and he stood up in front of the congregation. Later on, he started following Black Ice, which was another poet as well that gave Ricky Boone the push he needed.

Afterwards he joined a group on Facebook called The Inner Circle, which was ran by Kesha Murphy and king Judah. Both were erotic and love poets who asked Ricky to collaborate with them, which sparked a flame that drew him into a totally new audience. This eventually caused Ricky Boone to start writing out his emotions and experiences. "Through my marriages, whether it was on a positive or negative level, I figured why give up on love; because it hasn't given up on me. I started to desire certain things, wanting to share with that special person, and thought well...I know I can't be the only one who desires these things. By the end of my divorce in 2017, which I thought would have broken me, I learned to channel that pain into what I wanted in a woman, and how I wanted her to treat me. And that was the birth of my first book, pillow talk."

Now, Author Ricky Boone has taken his success to the next level, in urban erotica and drama.

   To learn more about Author Ricky Boone and his creatively written works and poetic expressions, visit the publishing website.

www.AJBPublishiing.com